MISTLETOE INN

JACQUIE BIGGAR

WAVEFRONT PUBLISHING

Crazy Little Thing Called Love

A touching, heartwarming story that takes your breath away.

Characters that will have you feeling so many emotions. It deals with family, misunderstandings, ranch life, horses, life long love and of course Pumpkin the cat.

Tony and Sophia's story had me laughing, crying and a bit frustrated with them at times. To me that is good writing when I can be moved to so many emotions while reading . The story is so good, I couldn't put it down.

— B

With This Heart

Such a sweet heartwarming romance about second chance love between two people who are obviously meant to be together. You won't want to put this story down until you're finished reading.

This is a wonderful series. Those of you who love military romance, wounded warrior romance and romantic suspense will love the stories written by this super talented, fabulous author!

— TAMMY

Maggie's Revenge

The first comment I can easily make here is: MAGGIE'S REVENGE punched my 'WOW' button!

Magdalena Holt goes rogue and deep undercover for the DEA... Fast forward: > Olga, a once teenage prostitute, and four others are captured by 'sex traffickers', put in a 'mud pit' basement. After several attempts, beatings, torture, and a lot of action, the group of five make their escape...

The suspense is staggering as 'Maggie' and her tattered and broken group valiantly withstand the vagaries of the Mexican compound and hell-hole, escape, and then await the DEA to recover them. Maggie wants to get home and bring down the most evil man she has ever known...a criminal and terrifying clown named Chenglei.

The romantic component in this exciting novel involves Maggie's partner and agency member, Adam O'Connor, who the boss fears will jeopardize rescue efforts because he is 'too close' - with his feelings for Maggie.

MAGGIE'S REVENGE is masterfully written and a 'must read' for the 'mystery and suspense' book lovers! The novel would also make a great movie! It's been a while since I've seen this 'theme' in movies...of course, I only watch an occasional TV movie.

— JULIE GEHRANDT

For my Family
Without them, I am nothing.

Tracy Petit won our Name the Movie contest with Fresh Fiction and would like to dedicate the story to her high school sweetheart and husband of almost thirty-five years, Bobby.
Passion is the springboard of a romance, but true love is the day-to-day support and companionship that bridges time.

Also, I want to dedicate this story to all those 'beasts' who feel themselves unworthy of a happy-ever-after.
You are beautiful.

True love stories never have endings.

— RICHARD BACH

INTRODUCTION

A grieving man finds the greatest gift is love in this heartwarming holiday romance.

Molly McCarty needs a new beginning after a disastrous divorce. When the opportunity to invest in a bed and breakfast appears online in Christmas, Michigan she's intrigued.

A snow storm derails her travels and leaves her at

the mercy of a grim stranger- who turns out to be her new partner!

Noah Kincaid loses his parents in a tragic fire that leaves him scarred inside and out. He's raised by a great-aunt and is devastated when cancer takes her life. But vowing never to care about anyone again is hampered by his troublesome new partner and her son.

Will a Christmas miracle bring three lonely hearts the gift of love?

MISTLETOE INN

USA TODAY BESTSELLING AUTHOR

JACQUIE BIGGAR

CHAPTER 1

olly McCarty white-knuckled the steering wheel of her compact car and peered through the blinding snow. The weatherman had forecast possible flurries later this evening. Not only was his timing wonky, but she'd passed the flurries halfway around the lake and was now into full-on whiteout conditions. The two-lane road had narrowed to one with deep ridges that threatened to pull her car into the steep banks. She'd followed a semi to the turn, but he'd disappeared into the hypnotic swirl and now she was on her own.

Her and Leo.

She hazarded a glance into the rearview mirror and was relieved to see her son sleeping, his head propped against the door with Teddy as a pillow. God, she wished she'd listened to her mother and waited to make

1

the trip. The chance of a fresh start had proven too big a temptation, and now they were in serious danger of going into the ditch and freezing to death. She gasped back a sob. The few sideroads they'd driven by looked worse than the one she was travelling on when the storm hit. If the lodge didn't appear in the next few miles she was going to have to assume they were lost, though with her car being white, she didn't think it would be a good idea to pull over and wait for the blizzard to end.

"Mommy, I don't feel so good," Leo's plaintive voice amped up her already tense nerves. He'd been complaining of a sore throat and tummy before falling asleep. She'd hoped the rest would help, but the raspy breathing suggested it was getting worse.

She glanced over her shoulder to see him rubbing his eyes and sniffling. "Use a tissue, honey. It won't be long now, I promise."

Please, be right. Please.

"That's what you said hours ago. I wanna go home," he whined.

Guilt reared its ugly head. If only she wasn't such a screw-up... "I know, baby, but think of this as a grand adventure, okay? Once we get to the lodge and all settled in, I'll run you a warm bath and we'll read your favorite storybook before bedtime. Does that sound good?"

"I guess," he said, his chubby arms holding Teddy close. "Why is it so dark out there? It's spooky."

The trees *were* unnerving in this muted light. Leo had been born in Edmonton, Alberta and raised in the suburbs. He'd never seen a world without streetlights before. One more reason why this was a good decision. But, she had to get them there safely to prove it.

"Where's Daddy? I want my daddy." He whimpered, the stress of leaving everything he knew and loved behind, combined with his illness, overwhelming.

Molly gritted her teeth and kept her gaze glued to the road when her heart ached to pull over and comfort her child. Even though they'd been divorced almost two years, Jason remained an active part of the family, his love for Leo undeniable. He'd understood her need to take this opportunity to move on, but he wasn't happy. She'd promised he could visit any time, and of course, Leo could stay with him during the holidays. She didn't want to consider how lonely she'd be during those absences.

Suddenly, a deer darted across the road only feet from the front of the car. Heart pounding, she hit the brakes and swerved, realizing too late that was a mistake in these icy conditions. The little car tried valiantly to hold the road, but the tires lost traction and then they were spinning out of control and heading straight for the towering dark forest rising up to meet them.

Molly screamed at Leo to hold on just before her head slammed into the steering wheel and everything went black.

CHAPTER 2

*N*oah Kincaid leaned on the shovel he'd been using to clear the driveway and took a breather. This was the third time today, and the snow showed no signs of letting up. If his new partner didn't make it soon, she wouldn't get through.

Wood smoke drifted on the crisp air and reminded him of the cozy fire waiting inside the big, old house he'd grown up in. It was still hard to believe his great-aunt was gone. She'd been a driving force in his life for so long, he didn't know what he was going to do without her. He could barely remember his parents. Aunty Betty had raised him after they'd died in the house fire that left him scarred down his left side.

"Blaze, where are you, boy?" He gave a sharp whistle and frowned when the groan of the forest was the only thing to answer him back. It wasn't like the

Shepherd to disappear when they were outdoors. Normally, he was right underfoot. "Blaze," he called again.

Damn dog, where was he?

There wasn't a lot of traffic that ever traveled up this road, but still... Blaze's dark coat blended into the shadows created by the giant spruce and pine trees. He'd hate to see his dog injured if he left him out here.

He sighed and lifted the collar of his winter jacket. Guess the fire could wait a few more minutes. "You're lucky I like you, dog," he said, trudging down the path he'd shoveled. Another inch or two had already come down, covering the toes of his sturdy boots. Normally, he enjoyed the outdoors this time of night. The snow danced around him while the silence welcomed introspection. Except, he didn't want to think about the past few months. The helplessness followed by anger, then resignation. His aunt had faced her future with quiet bravery and grace. Not him. He'd ranted against fate, the doctors, even God, for all the good it did. She was still gone, and he was once again alone.

"Blaze, I'm going to leave you out here for the wolves if you don't answer me," he shouted. His stomach did a nosedive. What if something *had* happened? Surely, he'd have heard his dog's cry for help. Nevertheless, he picked up his pace and whistled once more.

Suddenly, there was a faint yipping in the distance and Noah broke into a run, careful to keep to the side of the road where the snow wasn't packed down and slippery. He wouldn't be much help if he landed flat on his back. Blaze's excited yips grew louder and as he rounded a bend in the road he saw why. A small car had gone off the road and plowed into the snowbank, its front end crumpled like a sardine can.

Damn tourists, thinking they could handle winter conditions with summer tires and no experience.

As he drew closer he could see a dark shape slumped over the steering wheel and his pulse skyrocketed. Cell reception was poor on good days, in a storm like this...

"Okay, boy, I'm here. Settle down. You did good." He patted the dog's head and nudged him out of the way. "Let's see what we've got here." The shape hadn't moved at the sound of his voice, but the car was still running so he had to assume the person hadn't been there long.

He edged up the bank, using the wrecked vehicle to keep his balance and was almost to the driver's door when he heard a cry that froze his blood.

There was a child in the car.

He gave a last glance at the driver, then turned his attention to the back seat. He used his hand to clear the snow-covered window, then tugged his frozen gloves off with his teeth before digging into the deep pockets of his down jacket for the cell phone. Just as he thought, no bars. But, it did have a built-in flashlight and he used it to peer in through the back window.

A pale face with tear-streaked cheeks stared back at him, a teddy bear clutched in his arms.

"Hang on," Noah called, pasting what he hoped was a reassuring smile on his lips. "I'll have you out in no time." The boy gaped at him, eyes swimming with moisture. Noah tried the door, it refused to budge. He pointed to the lock, but the boy was scared and didn't move. There was no way Noah would be able to open the door without breaking the window.

"Listen," he said to the child, hoping he could hear through the glass. "I'm going to break this window. Can you hear me? I need you to cover your head."

No response.

He left the child and searched the ditch until he found a snow-covered boulder he deemed large enough to do the job. Blaze seemed to sense the boy's terror and stayed by the car, his nose pressed to the glass.

Noah carried the rock to the car, then called his dog. Blaze whined but did as he was commanded. As soon as he was clear, Noah hefted the rock and threw it at the window. It bounced off and went rolling into the ditch. He looked at the kid and made a motion to cover his own head, hoping he'd get the idea. It took a couple more tosses before there was a crash and the glass gave way.

He hurried over, reached in to flip the lock and opened the door. The interior light came on and he could feel the heat thanks to the car not stalling out after the crash, so at least they were warm. He brushed the glass off the seat and leaned in to check the kid, who had thrown the teddy bear over his head.

"You okay?" he asked, lowering the stuffed animal and doing a visual inspection of the child. A gash on the right cheek and a bump on his brow, but otherwise he seemed to be all in one piece. "Do you want to meet my dog? He loves kids." He had no idea if Blaze did or not. They'd never been around children much, but with the way the boy perked up, it was worth a shot. Blaze was as gentle as they came, the kid would be safe enough with him. "I'm just going to check on your parent, okay...? You got a name?"

"Leo," a timid voice replied. "But Mommy says I'm not 'posed to talk to strangers."

Noah's gaze went to the driver again. A woman then.

MOLLY CAME TO SLOWLY, Leo's voice coming to her through a fog. Her head and shoulders hurt worse than the time she'd gone skiing with Jason and lost her balance. She'd gone head over heels down the steep descent until the pole strapped to her wrist caught in the snow and dragged her to a halt. After Jason assured himself she was relatively unharmed he'd laughed and called her his Abominable Snow Girl.

"Ma'am, can you hear me? Are you injured?"

She stirred at the male voice coming from behind her seat, then wished she hadn't. *Ow, ow.* There'd been a deer, she remembered that much. She'd yelled at Leo to hold on, and then... *Leo.* She forced herself to lift her head, turning it carefully and blinking against the light coming from the back seat. What the...?

"Leo," she whispered, then cleared her throat to speak louder. "Leo, baby, are you okay?"

"He's fine." That voice again. "We're more concerned about you. Don't move, I'm coming around to your door now."

"There's a puppy, Mommy. He's licking my hand," Leo squealed.

Molly winced at the shrill pitch and shivered as cold air entered the car. A weight landed gently on her back and proceeded to lightly check her shoulder blades and spine before moving up to her neck and collarbone. She tried to turn and see who their rescuer was, but he stopped the motion.

"No, stay still until we know you haven't injured

your neck," he warned in a raspy undertone that raised goosebumps. "Your child is fine, a slight bump on the noggin, that's all. My dog is keeping him company. I'm going to see what I can find to fashion a collar for your neck and then we'll get you out of here. Sound good?"

Molly swallowed tears and gave a slight nod. She desperately wanted to hold her son, but that would have to wait. At least she could hear him chattering away in the back seat, it gave her a small measure of comfort.

"Y... yes, thank you," she told the stranger, grateful he'd happened along the stormy road. "D... do you live around here?" Shock was setting it, causing her teeth to chatter. She never had handled emergency situations very well.

"Just up the road a piece. Won't take long once we get you fixed up," he said absently from the rear seat. Strange that she missed the warmth and security of his hand on her back. "Here we go, this should work." He got out and came around to her door again, an imposing dark shape. "I'm going to wrap your son's scarf around your neck and use a book I found for a brace. Hang on."

He didn't give her any time to prepare, quickly getting the job done with a minimum of discomfort. "There," he said, then paused. "Your car isn't going anywhere, you hit that bank pretty hard. I'm going to run home and grab my vehicle. I'll be back before you know it, okay?" He waited until she nodded. "I'll leave Blaze, my dog, here for protection—though there's no reason you should need it, you're perfectly safe. Stay strong, okay, Mrs....?"

"McCarty. Molly. You can call me Molly," she murmured, her eyes fluttering closed.

He spoke loudly, she suspected on purpose. "Okay, Molly. You hang in there, you hear me? Hang on." He squeezed her arm, and then he was gone.

Blaze whined from the back seat and Leo crooned to him. "It's okay, puppy. Your daddy will save us and then me and mommy can come and stay at your house. Right, Mommy?"

Her forehead ached from resting against the hard plastic of the steering wheel. So much for their grand adventure. Jason and her mother would have a field day with this one. They were united in their faith that she was hopeless on her own. She'd so wanted to prove them wrong.

"Yes, honey. We can phone Grandma to come get us from there." Tears ran down her cheeks.

CHAPTER 3

The door creaked open, letting frigid air leak into the car. Molly jerked, then moaned. She must have passed out again. A sledgehammer had taken up residence in her head and it hurt to breathe, but at least she recalled where she was this time.

Leo coughed, then stage-whispered, "Mommy's sleeping."

She smiled and cringed, the motion exacerbating the pounding in her skull. "No, I'm not," she murmured, licking dry lips. It felt like a board was attached to her spine, and then she remembered the stranger who'd come to their rescue.

"Hello?" she asked, frustrated with her weakness. Headlights from another vehicle lit up the interior with a dull yellow glow, leaving the outside a solid black wall that seemed to press down on her car.

"How are you feeling?"

His breath tickled her ear. She tried to crane her head around to see him, but the pain to her right collarbone had her slumping in her seat. "Is my son hurt? I... I hit the bank hard. He was wearing his seatbelt, but please, can you just make sure he's okay?"

"Mommy, I have an owie on my forehead," Leo piped up from the back.

Oh, God. Please don't let anything happen to her baby. Please.

"It's nothing serious," the stranger said. "Looks like he bumped the window when you hit. He might end up with a shiner, though. You two will make a good pair."

She could feel him pushing against the back of her seat as he leaned across to Leo and tried not to panic. He was here to help. It would just be easier if she could put a face to the voice.

"Okay, champ," he said. "I undid your belt. Take my hand and walk across the seat. Can you do that? There's nothing to be afraid of. I'll carry you to my truck and you can wait there with Blaze until I get your mom out."

Blaze? He must mean the dog she'd heard whining just before the door opened. For some reason, that calmed her fears. He couldn't be all bad if he had a pet, right?

"Do as he says, honey. I'll be right behind you." She hoped.

Alone in the car and immobile, insecurities attacked. She'd dragged her son away from his safe, secure world and traveled across the country on the strength of a maybe. In the middle of a harsh Canadian winter. She needed her head examined.

Her car door opened and the stranger's outline blocked the light. "Ready?" he asked, leaning across to turn off the car and unbuckle her seatbelt. Molly sucked in a startled breath when the man's arm brushed her breast. "Sorry," he muttered.

Before she had time to digest the strange tingle his touch had wrought, he worked an arm under her legs and behind her back and lifted her free of the wreck. "Ugh," she whimpered, pain exploding as the blood rushed to her head.

"Shh." He gave her legs a gentle squeeze. "I've got you now. Hang on, we'll be home soon."

Every step jarred her aching body, so she concentrated on the hope he'd stirred. *Home.* She'd been so close... wait.

"Where... where are you taking us?" she whispered, shivering as he trudged through the snow.

He glanced down, his face in shadow. "The Mistletoe Inn. Don't worry, you're perfectly safe with me."

She frowned. Instead of the relief she should have felt, his words left a hollow in her stomach. Determined to rise above the strange reaction, she tried to smile, afraid it came out more like a grimace. "So, I was on the right road then. My son and I were hoping to make it before dark, but with the storm..."

"Only idiots are out in this weather," he growled.

Molly stiffened. "What does that make you then?"

His grip on her ribs tightened, and then they were at the truck and he was juggling to open the door without banging her head into the frame. The interior light came on, illuminating Leo and the big Shepherd he was clinging to. Her throat clenched. Her poor baby looked as though he'd gone a few rounds in the boxing ring. He had a puffy right eye that was already turning black and blue, and a cut above the eyelid crusted with dried blood.

"Blaze, in the back," the stranger ordered. The dog jumped the seat and filled the narrow bench behind Leo, his gaze reproaching. The man gently lowered Molly onto the seat and slid his arms free of her body. She bemoaned the loss of his heat.

Before he closed the door on her, she reached out and grabbed his arm, encased in a thick winter jacket. "Please, we'll need our bags. They're in the trunk."

He stared down at her hand until she snatched it back, then closed the door and trudged through the snow to get their luggage. She watched him for a moment, then shrugged off the awkward encounter and smiled at her son. "I guess Christmas pictures are out for Daddy and Grandma this year," she teased.

Leo laughed, as he was meant to. "You look funny," he agreed. "Do we have to go back to Grandma's now that our car is broken?"

Molly took his hand, marveling at her little boy's perceptiveness. "We might. We'll worry about that later, okay? How are you doing?" She brushed her fingers over his cut. "You have war wounds."

Leo felt the bump too but was more interested in the stranger making his way back to the truck, a suitcase under each arm. "He's really big, isn't he?"

Molly nodded, or as much as she could with a book strapped to her neck. "Yes. Lucky for us since he had to pack me over here like a sack of potatoes."

Leo giggled. "You're silly, Mommy." He hugged her arm.

She envied his resilience. She felt like she'd gone through his rock tumbling machine. "Love you, Boo."

"Love you, too," he muttered as the driver's door opened and the man slid into the cab.

He shot them a glance. "Bags are in the back. All set?"

"All set," Leo answered for them, sitting as tall as his three-foot frame would allow. Her little man.

"Just a minute," she said as he put the truck in gear. "We don't know your name."

He stepped on the gas, the back of the truck slipping sideways before it gained traction, leaving her car a snowbound mound on the side of the road. "Noah Kincaid. Your new partner."

Stunned, Molly gazed out the window at the swirling snow and wondered how her life had spun so out of control.

CHAPTER 4

*N*oah was acutely aware of the child and his mother, their bodies tense as the snow seemed to take aim at them, sending hypnotizing white bullets against the windshield.

"Is it always like this?" Molly asked, her voice shaky in the dark interior.

"Lake Superior isn't known for its moderate climate, Miss McCarty," he said, flicking a glance her way. Shock was a concern. He wanted to get her and the kid inside the house before the storm got worse. "What did you expect when you accepted the offer to move to Christmas, Michigan?"

She choked out a laugh. "Something a bit more romantic? Snowmen and elves and mistletoe, maybe. And it's Ms.," she added.

She was married. Good. Easier, since they would

be sharing a house. "Is your husband joining you for Christmas?" If so, he'd make himself scarce. He had no interest in seeing their homecoming celebration.

"That's unlikely, we're divorced," she said, and shifted as though uncomfortable with the conversation. "Why did you need a partner, Mr. Kincaid? You seem less than pleased to have us here."

She had that right. "My aunt wanted you, not me." She could take that however she liked.

"Oh, I get it." The humor in her voice rankled. "You don't seem the social butterfly type."

"Hell, no," he muttered, slanting a glance at his passengers. "Sorry, not used to kids." Leo was staring outside, mesmerized by the falling snow. Molly's gaze was focused on Noah, and she turned away when he caught her, as though embarrassed.

"Leo knows not to use bad words, but don't be surprised if he doesn't come after you to donate to the swear jar. He's saving for a bicycle. I'm trying to break the habit, too," she admitted.

With her wavy blond hair and blue eyes to rival the midnight sky, Molly looked more like an angel than a lowly human with faults. Knowing she had to occasionally add to her son's cussing jar made her more approachable. Not that it mattered, she was here to do a job, nothing more.

"I can't wait to meet your aunt," Molly said,

unaware of the knife she'd just twisted in his heart. "We talked often on the phone. She seems kind."

She was. He didn't know where he'd have been without her. Nowhere good, that's for sure. "My aunt is dead." He frowned at her gasp. "Didn't our lawyer fill you in before you left?" The driveway came up on the right and he took the turn carefully, aware of the layer of ice under the snow waiting to trip up the unwary. They didn't need any more accidents tonight.

"No." Molly's voice was faint. "When did she... um, pass away?"

"Ten days ago," he answered flatly. It still hurt to think about her laying in that hospital bed, pale and unbearably frail. Cancer was a bitch that stole his aunt's health from the inside out and there wasn't a damn thing anyone could do about it.

"I'm so sorry," Molly murmured. "Were you close?"

He clenched the steering wheel. "Yeah."

They pulled up in front of the inn and he shut off the truck. The lamp in the den cast a soft glow through the window, highlighting the falling snowflakes piling up on the Weigela bushes in giant cotton balls. Layers of snow clung to the clapboard siding leaving the old building dressed for company like a grande dame with glittering icicles hanging from the eaves for earrings. He loved this old house. When his aunt had first come up with the idea for a bed and breakfast, he'd balked. The idea of waking up to strangers and having to make nice did not appeal, but his aunt was adamant and for the most part it had worked out well. He'd done the maintenance and she'd cooked the meals and socialized with the guests. It had given her a reason to fight the disease depriving her body of strength.

Noah opened the door and dropped lightly onto the ground, compacting the snow beneath his feet. He turned and looked at his passengers. The kid stared at him with big eyes and for a moment, Noah thought he could see his scars, but the night's shadows were his friend. The shock would come later, once they were inside the house and he had nowhere to hide.

"C'mere, kid. I'll help you down, then carry your mom inside."

Leo checked with his mother first. Only when she smiled and gave him a reassuring nod, did he scramble across the seat and accept Noah's hand. The feeling of small fingers grasping his thumb moved something in his breast and he coughed to rid himself of the sensation. "Where's your mitts?" he asked gruffly, frowning at the snow.

"I couldn't find them," the boy said, and used Noah's hand as leverage to jump from the truck. The feathery light flakes floated up, then settled over his red lightning bolt boots in a downy blanket. He took in the scene with wide eyes. "Can I make a snowman?"

Noah's rusty laugh surprised himself as much as the kid. "Maybe later. We better see to your mother first."

Leo sighed, his breath creating little cloud puffs in the frosty air. "Ookay," he half-heartedly agreed. He gave a last wistful glance at the piled snowbank along the driveway, then trudged around the vehicle, his head not much taller than the tires.

Noah followed the miniature tracks and picked up his pace when the passenger door creaked open. "Stay..." *there*, he'd been about to say when two nylon-clad legs appeared wearing knee-length black leather boots with sensible heels. Molly slid from the cab and would have crumpled if not for his quick reflexes. She gasped as he grabbed her waist and tugged her up against his body. She looked at him with startled eyes and he stilled, waiting for the moment when her expression changed to horror.

Instead, she knocked him sideways by smiling.

CHAPTER 5

One moment Molly was falling and the next she was snuggled up against a living, breathing brick wall. She sucked in a surprised breath and inhaled a tantalizing mix of pine and citrus. Disarmed, she looked up to thank her rescuer once again, and stilled, arrested by the stark beauty of his face.

Up until now the evening skies had kept much of her new partner in shadows, but the lights from inside the house spilled over his rangy frame and she realized just how big he was. She stood almost five-nine in her boots and he still towered over her with broad shoulders and strong arms holding her against his chest. Dark, shaggy hair brushed the collar of his parka and a widow's peak highlighted a broad, lined forehead under his cap. Glittering eyes dared her to comment on the jagged scar running down the left side of his face from cheek to neck, but all she could focus on was the fascinating quirk it gave to his upper lip, like he was smiling at something funny.

So, she smiled back.

He frowned and dropped his arms, stepping back a pace. "I *said* I'd carry you," he grumbled.

He reminded her of Leo when he didn't get his way.

"I'm perfectly able to walk into the house," Molly said tartly, though now she wasn't so sure. At least she knew her neck and collarbone weren't as bad as she'd first thought. They ached but she could move. Or she could if she got rid of Leo's book tied to her head. She reached up to untie the scarf and wobbled in her boots.

Noah grabbed her again, a beleaguered expression taking over his face. Before she could react, he lifted her into his arms like a newborn babe and nodded to Leo. "Get the door, kid. It's unlocked."

Leo's eyes grew big, no doubt astonished at seeing his mother in a stranger's arms—though he didn't seem like a stranger. "Go ahead, son. Mr. Kincaid is practicing his chivalry."

Leo looked puzzled by the adult word, then shrugged and headed for the house. Noah, on the other hand, had a bit more to say.

"Are you mocking me, Ms. McCarty?" He stared at

her with an inscrutable look and she barely avoided squirming, uncomfortable with the close proximity of that compelling mouth.

"It's Molly," she admonished. "Sorry. I'm used to speaking to a five year old."

"Do I look five to you?" he asked, amusement sparking in those dark eyes.

Umm, nope. If there was one thing she knew for sure, the hard, masculine chest beneath her breast was *not* that of a child.

He let her get away with her silence and followed Leo up to the house, whistling for Blaze to come. The big dog appeared without a sound and waited patiently for the door to open. Leo used two hands to turn the knob and then they were thrust inside on a rush of cold air. Molly's head swam as Noah kicked off his boots and carried her through the foyer and down a short hall to a den lit by warm Tiffany lamps and a glowing fireplace that made her skin tingle.

He set her down on a faded brocade sofa and knelt at her feet to tug off her boots, one leg at a time. Molly blushed at the intimacy and brushed his fingers away.

"I'm not an invalid," she snapped.

His brows slid into his hairline and he leaned back, hands in the air. "Maybe not, but you *are* injured. I was simply trying to help," he said calmly before rising to tend to the fire.

Leo stared at her with uncertain eyes, and she gave him a reassuring smile. It wasn't his fault. The day was catching up to her and she wasn't handling it well. She lifted her arm, ignoring the twinge in her neck, and invited him to come sit with her. "I need a cuddle. It's been a long day."

He ran over and buried his face in her armpit. She hugged him close and breathed in his little boy scent.

"Hey now, what's that for?" she asked, glancing at Noah's broad back bent over the fire. Leo mumbled something, but she couldn't make it out. "What's that, honey? I can't hear you."

He looked up at her with teary, overtired eyes. "I *said*, did Bambi's mommy die?"

Oh, no.

In all the confusion after the accident, she'd forgotten what caused it in the first place. She stared at her son's unhappy face, lost for words. Just the thought of that poor animal laying in a cold ditch twisted her stomach into knots.

"The deer is fine, kid." Noah returned the poker to its stand and peeled the dark gray parka from his shoulders.

Molly's mouth went dry.

"How do *you* know?" Leo asked, his nose in the air.

"Leo," Molly chastised. "That's not the way you speak to people. Apologize, young man."

Blaze whined at her tone, rose from his bed by the fireplace and paced over to lay his big head on Leo's knee, looking up at him with soulful brown eyes.

"Sorry," he mumbled, rubbing the dog's fuzzy ears.

Noah shrugged and hung his coat over one of two club chairs positioned near the fire. "Don't worry about it. The deer ran just as I got there thanks to Blaze's warning. You two are lucky it wasn't more serious. Your car is going to be down for a while, by the look of it."

Oh, no. The rest of their bags were in the car. Molly gazed at her damp dress in dismay. "But, our clothes," she stammered.

"The car isn't going anyplace. I'll bring them up to the house in the morning when I go to meet the tow truck." Noah's gaze ran over her body. "You can wear something of mine for tonight if the luggage in the truck doesn't have what you need."

Even though she'd been married for ten years, his words made her flush. "Thank-you," she said, and tried not to think of his shirt against her skin. "Is there a body shop in town then?"

He nodded. "Christmas ain't big, but it's got about everything a person could need. We'll be getting busy soon. Tourists love to visit Santa's workshop, and then there's the Light Up Parade and holiday dance." He paused and sank into a chair with a sigh. "We go all out for the tourists during the winter season, we need the business to keep the town alive."

She could understand that. Her job in the hospitality industry had shown how much people valued their getaways. It was the main reason she'd made the decision to sink her finances into this project. But, she hadn't planned on Noah.

Noah leaned back and rested his weary body against the plush softness of his aunt's favorite chair. He could remember many evenings spent in the den listening to her soft voice asking him about his day. She'd always shown a real interest in his thoughts and aspirations. After the fire and his parents' death, he'd been angry at the world. She'd visited him at the hospital, even though he refused to speak, and when it was time for him to leave, he'd come here—to the inn.

He stared at Molly and fancied the fire was caught in the gold of her hair, turning it into a shimmering halo as she bent over to speak to her son. Though her injuries were worse than Leo's, she'd ignored them to make sure he was safe. Molly McCarty was a good mother.

"Looks like he's giving up on us." He smiled as Leo fought the valiant fight to keep his eyes open.

Molly kissed his brow, only wincing a little. "He's been a trooper through all of this. We drove for five days to get here and he never once complained."

Noah recalled his aunt mentioning she lived in Alberta. "Why drive? A plane would have been faster, safer too in the winter." He didn't have to say she was a female on her own, she must have read it in his eyes.

"Are you a chauvinist, Mr. Kincaid?"

He almost grinned at the indignant tone of her voice. "No, ma'am. I'm a realist. I'd wager you haven't changed very many tires on the side of a busy highway in twenty below weather." He sat up to make his point. "And even if you have, you're still vulnerable just by virtue of being a female. It's a dangerous world out there, Molly. You can't always trust strangers to help."

"Like you?" she snapped, on the offensive. Then she sighed. "I'm sorry, that was uncalled for. You're right. In hindsight it was probably not the wisest decision."

"You made it. That's the main thing." He was surprised by how much it mattered to him. He barely knew this woman and her son, and he sure as hell didn't want to be concerned about them. Everyone he'd cared about was gone.

"Thanks to you." She met his gaze and something intimate passed between them.

Noah cleared his throat and stood. "Tomorrow's

going to be a big day. Want me to carry the little guy to bed?"

She looked down at Leo who'd fallen asleep against her chest. "Please. Can you recommend a doctor for him? I'm worried about that bump on his forehead."

"Sure. My aunt's family doc is great. I'm sure he'll see *both* of you." He stared pointedly at her collarbone.

She smiled, and butterflies swirled in his stomach. "Thanks for everything, Noah. Let's start fresh tomorrow, okay?"

When she smiled like that he was ready to agree to anything she asked. He was in so much trouble.

CHAPTER 6

*M*olly woke to the aroma of bacon and toast the next morning. She rolled over and bumped into Leo. He might only be three feet tall, but he still managed to take up most of the queen-size pedestal bed. The down comforter was feather light, the mattress thick and plush. She felt like a princess in the traditionally styled bedroom. A chiffonier with an old-fashioned mirror filled a nook. Her purse rested on top of a six-drawer dresser with intricately scrolled woodwork and a white and red crocheted runner to match the bedding. Shiplap gave texture to the walls, and warm oak planking covered the floor. Their luggage sat by the door. She flushed, remembering her host showing up at the door with the bags last night. As aloof as he'd seemed, they would have been lost without his help. It was apparent he'd been close to his aunt and missed her. She wondered about his scars. The disfigurement served to add interest to a strong face. They didn't bother her, but she could tell by the way he kept his face averted, it did him.

She brushed her son's bangs back and was relieved to see the swelling had come down on his forehead. The cut seemed to be mending nicely under the butterfly bandage Noah had applied to the injury, but the bruising was worrisome.

She left Leo sleeping and rose, grimacing at her disheveled appearance in the beveled mirror. Her hair lay flattened against the right side of her head while the left looked as though she'd stuck her finger in a light socket. Attractive. At least she had a change of clothes.

"Bathroom is at the end of hall," Noah had revealed last night as he showed them to their room. He'd nodded toward an open door on the opposite side and two rooms down.

She'd wanted to ask where he slept but thought it might seem too forward. "Thank you. For everything. When I think what could have happened…"

"But didn't."

His voice sent a quiver to her belly. She'd looked up and lost herself in his dark eyes. "No, it didn't. Thank the Lord."

Noah blinked and took a step back, breaking the

spell. "I don't think *He* had much to do with it. I'll see you in the morning." He'd strode away, leaving her to wonder if he was as disillusioned as he seemed.

Molly found clean clothes for Leo and a cranberry red sweater and blue jeans for herself—no socks though, they must be in her other bags—and after a last glance at her sleeping son, eased the door open and hurried down the short hall to the washroom. Rather than the soothing bath her body craved, she hurried through a quick shower, combed towel-damp hair back with her fingers and called it good enough—that coffee was calling her name.

She followed her nose and found the kitchen on the main floor of the house. Noah stood at the counter, cup in hand, staring at the winter wonderland beyond the window. Hoar frost coated evergreen trees in sparkling splendor against a brilliant blue sky while the freshly fallen snow blanketed the yard in a pillowy white cloud. There would be no containing Leo once he woke up.

"Is that coffee I'm smelling?" she asked, smiling at the startled look on Noah's face. "Sorry, I guess you didn't hear me clomping through your home."

He gave her a skeptical glance and set his cup down in order to reach another out of the cupboard by the farmhouse sink. "There's not enough of you *to* clomp." He set the mug under the brewer and added a pod to the machine. Soon, heaven began to pour into the cup. He pointed to the platter of pancakes, bacon and toast piled high on top the gas stove. "Help yourself. I figured you might wake up with an appetite this morning." He opened another cupboard, removed a couple of plates and set them on the counter. "How's the neck?"

Molly edged closer, drawn as much by the man as the food. She thought briefly of looking for a fork, then shrugged and snagged a slice of bacon with her fingers. Her eyes closed at the first bite, the better to savor the smoky sweetness of the cured meat.

"This is delicious," she moaned, licking her lips. "Who taught you to cook?" Her ex-husband couldn't even boil water. She opened her eyes to see him staring at her mouth, his gaze intense.

Her pulse fluttered, sending heat spiraling through her chest and lower. Rattled, she reached for her coffee at the same time he went to hand it to her and the hot liquid splashed his fingers.

"Oh my gosh, I'm so sorry," she gasped. "Here, get some cold water on it before it blisters." She leaned past him to turn on the tap, his hard bicep brushing her cheek. When he didn't move she reached out, took the hot cup from his hand, grasped his wrist near an intricately woven black and pink bracelet, and guided his reddened fingers beneath the spray.

He flinched and let out what she was pretty sure was a curse under his breath. "Are you accident prone, Ms. McCarty, or just bad luck?"

Molly pursed her lips and stepped back to let him tend to his own injury—grumpy man. "The water should help. I'll check on Leo. What time did you want to head into town?"

He sighed and turned off the tap to open a drawer for a striped dishtowel to dry his hand. "After lunch. They should have the road plowed by then. I went down early this morning and helped the tow truck load your car. It doesn't look as bad as it did last night. He thinks Arties can have it up and running by Christmas."

"Arties?"

He nodded. "A collision shop in town. They do good work. You're in safe hands."

Her gaze was drawn to the bracelet on his arm. "What does that mean?"

He glanced down at the braided cord and a shadow passed over his face. "I had it made after my aunt died. The pink is for cancer, and the black signifies..." He fingered the band, then threw the towel at the counter before sweeping past her. "Be ready by one or I'll leave without you," he said, and disappeared down the hall. A moment later she heard the back door bang shut.

Molly leaned over the counter to search outside the window, but there was no sign of him. She picked up her coffee and took a sip, grimacing at the tepid temperature. Or maybe it was simply the emptiness in the room that left a bad aftertaste.

CHAPTER 7

*N*oah waited impatiently while the grocery clerk rang up his items. His cheeks heated as the woman at the till eyed the feminine products with a raised brow. In a town the size of Christmas there weren't many secrets, and everyone knew he lived alone.

"Just stocking up ahead of the guests we have arriving next week," he told Mrs. Nabors.

She placed a hand on an ample hip. "You need some help out there, Noah, dear? My Jessabelle left her good-for-nothing husband and could sure use a job. She's been staying with me and Davy. We don't mind or nothing, but it would sure help us at Christmas if there was another paycheck coming in, if you know what I mean?"

Reluctantly, he nodded. "Tell her to give me a call

and we'll figure something out." What else could he say? He'd dated Jessie in high school. She'd gotten a raw deal with that loser she'd married.

"Bless your sweet heart, Noah Kincaid. Your darlin' auntie would be so proud of you." She gifted him with a mile-wide smile and squeezed his hand as she dropped the change into his open palm. "This means the world to Davy and me. Anything you need, just ask, you hear me now?"

Embarrassed, he nodded and hefted the paper bags into his arms. "Yes, ma'am, I'll do that," he said, shouldering the heavy glass door open.

A blast of frigid air made him grateful for the Sherpa wool lining his thick denim jacket. He hurried to his truck angle-parked halfway down the block and stored the groceries on the back seat. Locking the door, he lifted the collar of his coat as a meager protection from the wind and jumped the snow bank lining the curb to cross the street and make his way over to the Roasted Chestnut Café.

The scent of fried onions and coffee greeted him as he entered. His mouth watered. He didn't come in often, but that didn't stop people calling out a greeting as he clumped through the restaurant in his winter boots. He acknowledged a few of his neighbors, but his focus was on the woman and child waiting for him.

She was beautiful, her lustrous blond hair a perfect

foil for midnight blue eyes and alabaster skin. A fairy-tale princess come to life. Then she tapped her watch and glowered, and he grinned. His princess had teeth.

"You're late," she sniped as he slid into the booth across from her. "I... we were getting worried."

The kid barely glanced up, his attention on the leaning tower of creamer he'd built. Noah raised a brow. "Did you eat already?"

She shook her head and her hair made a shushing sound against the red nylon of her ski jacket. "We were waiting for you." She sipped her coffee—black, the way he liked it—and set her cup down. "Everything okay?"

Shoot. He was supposed to be finding alternative transportation while their car was in the repair shop. He'd been in such a rush to meet them he'd forgotten.

"Yeah, sure," he said, turning his cup up for the smiling waitress. He waited until she stepped away to continue. "Listen, my truck is usually at home. Why don't you and the boy use it until yours is ready? It's a four-by-four, better for our winter roads." He didn't add safer with her shaky driving record, but she must have seen it in his eyes.

She crossed her arms and leaned back in the booth. "If you're sure you trust me with your baby, then thank you. I hope it won't be for more than a few days, I have lots to do if we want to be ready for the holidays."

Noah frowned. "Such as?" He'd picked up the groceries and shoveled the drive. What else was there?

Molly glanced from him to her son's creamer tower and back to him as though he should be able to figure it out. Then, it dawned on him what she was getting at and he shook his head. "No. We are *not* getting a tree."

His aunt had loved Christmas. She'd decorated the house from top to bottom, inside and out. He closed his eyes, imagining the scents of gingerbread, chocolate, rosemary and sage. He wasn't ready to face the holiday without her just yet. His heart clenched. Maybe never.

"But, where will Santa put the presents if we don't have a Christmas tree?" the little kid piped up.

Molly's gaze warmed with empathy. She squeezed Leo's shoulders and gave him a kiss on the forehead. "Santa Claus won't let a little old thing like a tree stop him from delivering gifts—as long as you're a good boy, that is."

The waitress appeared at the table and gave them a friendly smile. "If you're looking to buy a tree, my uncle has the best selection. He's right on the edge of town, by the library." She pulled a card out of her apron and handed it to Noah. "Tell him I sent you— Tammy—he'll give you a good deal."

She filled their coffee cups, then set the glass carafe on the table, pen poised to take their order. "Have you decided on what you'd like to eat?"

"Pizza," Leo chimed in.

Tammy laughed. "I like a man who knows what he wants," she teased.

Molly rubbed the top of her kid's head. "Manners, mister."

"Ok. *Please*," he added before going back to making buttermilk out of the creamers.

Noah reached out and gathered a few, putting them in the bowl. "Molly?" he asked, conscious of a frisson of awareness at the sound of her name on his lips.

She closed the menu and handed it to Tammy. "I'll try your homemade hamburger soup and dinner bun combo, *please*," she said, stressing the courtesy term with a side-glance at her son.

Tammy nodded. "Great choice, it's a local favorite." She turned to Noah. "And for you?"

Noah was hungry enough to eat one of everything, but he settled their all-day breakfast selections. "Steak and eggs. Steak medium rare, eggs over easy."

Tammy wrote his request in her little notebook, then picked up the coffee pot. "Thank you, it shouldn't take too long. We're in between rushes right now."

They were quiet for a few moments after the waitress moved on to the next table, chattering with the customers like they were old friends. People laughed, seniors were shooting the breeze. He'd always been an introvert, but the last few months, caring for his aunt, he'd been touched by the kindness of the community. They'd stepped in with fundraisers, companionship when she needed it the most, casseroles—his freezer was stocked for the next six months—and sympathy. So much compassion that he'd closed himself off from it, the reason too painful to bear.

But now, sitting in this booth with a beautiful woman, listening to the happiness surrounding them, he could hear his aunt's voice in his head.

Life's too short, son. Don't go wasting it mourning for things that can't be changed. Live, baby boy. Live.

He fingered the card the waitress had laid on the table. "We'll take a drive past the tree farm on our way home," he said, abruptly. "Can't hurt to look."

Leo clapped with glee, his smile lighting up the room.

Molly's was softer, but no less warm. "No," she agreed. "It can't hurt at all."

CHAPTER 8

*M*olly hurried to keep up as Leo wove in and out of the evergreens on display, the air tinted with the scent of pine and balsam. His childish laughter warmed her heart. He was unhappy leaving Alberta and his family behind. She couldn't blame him. Ever since her divorce from Jason, she'd been coasting, searching for... well, she wasn't really sure. She just knew it wasn't in Edmonton. That was her past, Christmas was her future.

Or, so she hoped.

"Leo, where are you?" she called, half laughing, half worried. The fairy lights strung in graceful arcs across the large gazebo-type structure were pretty, but they didn't make finding a little boy in a dark jacket easy. Nearby couples glanced in her direction, then joined in the search. It wasn't that big an area, but there were a lot of hiding places a mischievous little boy might discover.

"I've got him." Noah strode out from between two thick conifers with Leo in his arms. He looked like an outdoor magazine model with his lived-in face and burly shoulders. Molly heard the appreciative sighs from the women around her and her heart stuttered. He really was a handsome man.

She thanked the searchers and shook her head as Noah reached her side. "He was there one minute and then he was gone. You seem to be making a habit out of coming to our rescue."

He gazed at her with those dark eyes, his hair ruffled by the chilly breeze, and she had the strongest urge to reach up and kiss those uncompromising lips. He'd probably think she was crazy. She'd have to be to try. He hadn't given any sign of a mutual attraction, and besides, they barely knew each other.

"He was chasing after a puppy. I'm sure he's sorry he worried you." He nodded to Leo. "Better apologize to your mother, now."

Leo looked at her, excitement sparkling in his eyes. "Mommy, you gotta come see. The puppy is so cute. He's as white as snow and has blue eyes. Can I have him, Mommy. *Please.*" He kicked his booted feet, narrowly missing Noah's groin. Noah winced and set him down.

Molly gave him an apologetic glance, then crouched beside her son. "Honey, you need to calm down. First, Noah is right. You should say sorry for disappearing the way you did. That's a dangerous thing to do, and I don't expect you to do it again. *Capisci*?"

Chastened, Leo scuffed his feet in the snow. "Capease."

Molly bit her lip on a smile. "Second, you'd better say thank you to Mr. Kincaid for helping me find you."

He tipped his head and looked way up at the giant of a man watching them with unfathomable eyes. "Thank you, Mr. Kincaid," he said dutifully. Then his gaze went to the trees. "Can we go see the puppy now?"

"Leo...," Molly warned.

He gazed at her with a woebegone expression. "Please, Mom. I'll be good, I promise."

Molly rose, accepting the hand Noah held out for support. "I thought we were here to look at Christmas trees. Mr. Kincaid was nice enough to bring us out, but I'm sure he has other things he'd like to do, so let's just stick to the plan, okay?"

His bottom lip quivered, but he nodded and stuck his gloved hand in her free one. And that's when she realized she was still holding Noah's hand. She dropped it like a hot coal, then flushed at the glint in his eyes.

Time for a distraction.

"So, are you a Charlie Brown tree sort of person, or do you like the big, thick ones that fill up the living room?"

"How about starting somewhere in the middle?" he said, his mouth quirking in that mesmerizing smile again.

Yeah. Meeting in the middle was beginning to sound just right.

NOAH COULDN'T BELIEVE he'd been talked into choosing a Christmas tree. He'd known he'd have to decorate the house some for his guests, but a tree... It would stir up memories he wasn't sure he was ready to cope with. His aunt had loved the holidays. She'd even made an angel for the top of the tree and his job had been to place it and do the lights each year. He'd hated those jumbled lights. It took him an hour just to unscramble the mess before he could begin the process of stringing. And there was a certain way to do that arduous chore. His aunt insisted the lights needed to circle the tree, hitting every branch if she had her way. She'd turn on the stereo and hum to the carols and he'd try his best to do as she asked without falling off the ladder and landing in her blasted tree.

Funny thing was, he'd give anything to go back to those days now.

"Look, this one is perfect," Molly called, her hands doing a Vanna White beside the ugliest balsam fir he'd ever seen.

Its branches were lopsided, and the top had a crooked hook, but he took one look at the glow on her face and nodded. "Yep, it'll do." Her smile tugged him closer. He lifted his hand to brush her cheek. "You're beautiful when you smile," he murmured, mesmerized by her expressive eyes.

"Kiss," someone yelled.

"Kiss her," another voice said.

Startled, Noah turned to see they'd drawn a crowd. They pointed above Molly's head, big Cheshire grins chasing across their faces. Already guessing what he'd see, Noah glanced up. Sure enough, mistletoe had been tied to the fairy lights.

He looked at Molly and could see the mix of embarrassment and understanding. She was about to give him an out, he knew it, but suddenly that's not what he wanted.

He stepped back into her space, tipped her chin, and slowly, slowly—giving her time to stop what was surely insanity—he laid his lips to hers and closed his eyes, lost in a slew of sensations bombarding him all at once. Heat. Texture. She tasted of the coffee they'd drank and the apple pie they'd had for dessert. He wanted to consume her. Desire turned him deaf to the crowd, there was only Molly. Her smooth skin beneath his lips, the feel of her arms snaking around his neck, her curvy body fitting him in all the right places. He hummed with the need to get this woman in his bed.

He broke the kiss, panting hard and leaned his forehead against hers, shocked by the depth of his response. Now that his pulse was settling he could hear the clapping and hooting and hollering going on behind them. He grimaced.

"You okay?" he asked, lifting his head.

She stared up at him with a dazed expression. "Huh? Oh yeah, sure." She backed away, almost tripping over the ugly tree. "I... I'd better take Leo for that hot chocolate I promised him when we pulled up. Can you handle the tree?"

Space between them wasn't going to erase what just happened, but he let her go with a nod, ignoring the sigh from the crowd. He stood there as they dispersed, him and that damn ugly tree, the familiar loneliness an unwanted ache in his chest.

CHAPTER 9

*M*olly sipped cocoa with Leo and luxuriated in the warmth of a roaring bonfire. Chatting customers milled around the extensive snack table, enjoying butter tart squares, Nanaimo bars, pumpkin pie squares, and shortbread cookies for one dollar apiece. She'd opted for a cookie for herself and a Nanaimo bar for Leo. She'd be lucky to get him to sleep before midnight with all the extra sugar and excitement but didn't really mind. After the chaotic move, this downtime was needed.

Besides, Christmas was only a couple of weeks away.

"Have you written your list for Santa?" she asked her son, swiping the chocolate on his lip with a napkin. "There's not much time. We need to get it mailed to the North Pole, remember."

Leo ducked away from her ministrations and stuffed the last bite into his mouth. "Wha... if 'e can't read my writing?"

"Don't talk with your mouth full," she reprimanded. "Santa can read all the children's wishes, and there's nothing wrong with your printing anyway. You do a fine job with your letters."

His father had pestered him to try harder over everything. It had been a big bone of contention between them. After all, Leo was only five. He wasn't even in school yet and already knew his ABC's. Jason needed to let the kid be a kid. There was plenty of time for him to excel in his studies.

"Well, hello there." A pleasant-looking man with a flowing white beard in faded coveralls and a logger's jacket smiled down at Leo. "I see you found my wife's magic hot chocolate. We get people from three counties over driving here just to fill up their thermoses, you know." His eyes twinkled with good humor. "Have you seen my puppies yet? They're running around here somewhere. Probably gettin' themselves into mischief. They like to nip at scarves and mitts." He held up his own gloves to show the pulled threads and teeth marks in the leather fingers.

Leo's eyes grew big. "There was more than one?" he asked, completely overlooking the whole biting thing.

JACQUIE BIGGAR

"Ho, ho, ho, oh yes!" The jolly man chortled. "Ol' Maisey gave birth to nine of the critters. It's hard to keep track of 'em all." He patted his rotund belly.

"Don't let Chris talk you into taking one of our puppies." A gray-haired matron with rosy cheeks joined them. "He's bound and determined they have to be gone by Christmas, or else..."

"Or else what?" Leo whispered, his mouth hanging in awe.

Molly was a little tongue-tied herself. If she didn't know better... "I imagine you won't have any trouble finding homes. The pup we saw was beautiful." She glanced around the fire to see if anyone else found the couple... well, strange. But no one paid them any mind. It was as though they were in their own little world.

Where the heck was Noah?

"They are a handsome lot," Chris agreed. "It's just that the bigger they get, the more they eat. Soon, me and Mary here won't be able to feed ourselves. And as you can see, I like my food." He chuckled and rubbed his tummy.

"We could make flyers and hand them out to our guests," Molly suggested. "I'm a new partner at a bed and breakfast in town. Maybe you've heard of it, the Mistletoe Inn?"

"Oh." Mary clasped her hands to her substantial

bosom. "The Kincaid place. We were so very sorry for Noah's loss. Betty was a long-standing customer of ours. Always bought the Douglas fir. Said it reminded her of her childhood." Mary dragged a tissue from her pocket and dabbed her eyes. "She did a lot for the community, and for that handsome nephew of hers, poor boy. After the fire... well, it was a tough time for the both of them, it was."

"Fire?" Molly knew she was treading dangerous ground, but the urge to learn more about her enigmatic partner won out.

Chris drew a squiggly line down his cheek. "Noah was little more than a boy at the time. The fire started in the attic. He did everything he could to save them, but his parents didn't stand a chance. By the time emergency crews arrived the right side of the house was engulfed, and he lay unconscious on the stairs. Another few minutes and..."

Embers popped sending a shower of sparks into the air. Molly gasped. She'd been so caught up in the tale she'd forgotten where they were for a moment. Poor Noah. She couldn't imagine the pain he'd gone through. And to lose his family that way... horrible, just horrible.

"Mommy, is that why Mr. Kincaid has a creepy face?" Leo asked.

Molly frowned. "Mr. Kincaid's face is *not* scary.

And you know better than to make those kinds of comments, young man."

"Leave him be, the kid's just telling it like he sees it." Noah appeared out of the dark, his eyes glinting in the firelight.

Embarrassed on her son's behalf and drawn to the pain she sensed hovering under Noah's tough façade, Molly held out the shortbread wrapped in a white paper doily. "I bought you a cookie." As peace-offerings went, it was sadly lacking, but she held her breath until he accepted it, nonetheless.

He nodded toward the elderly couple. "Guess I don't need to ask who did the baking. Mary's sweets are famous in these parts."

"I can understand why, these are fabulous." Molly smiled. "We could use someone with your talent at the inn." Darn her impulsiveness, she had no idea whether they could afford to be hiring out or not. She chanced a glance at Noah and was relieved to see him nodding his head.

"She's right. I should have thought of it sooner. Any chance we could talk a deal on morning pastries, Mary?" He finished his cookie and balled up the wrapper before tossing it into the flames. Leo watched with wide-eyed wonder as the paper doily caught fire and burned a bright blue until it disintegrated.

Chris and Mary seemed to negotiate a private conversation with their eyes, then Chris held out his hand. "Tell you what, this is a right busy time of the year for me and I ain't getting any younger. If you could see your way to delivering a few of these here trees, Mary and I would be right obliged. She always bakes more than she can sell in the Sweet Shop. I'm sure she'd be willing to set aside a tray or two for your guests." He waited for Mary's beaming smile. "Do we have a deal?"

Noah grasped the other man's hand and shook. "We do."

"Well, good. Now we have that sorted out, did you decide on your Christmas tree?"

Noah met Molly's gaze and a warmth that had nothing to do with the fire heated her chest. "Yes, sir. Molly picked out a special tree. It's going to look just fine once we get it decorated." He nudged Leo. "I'm going to need your help, okay?"

Leo held his ground, though she could see the big man intimidated him. "Sure," he said. "Mommy doesn't let me hang the balls though, she says it's dangerous."

Noah raised his brow. "Well, I think I have some you can handle. They're collectibles though, so you need to be careful. My aunt bought a new one every year, and she saved some I made as a kid."

"Cool." Leo turned to Molly. "Can I make a ball for the tree? Please, Mommy?"

She laughed. "Look what you started now." Her smile encompassed the adults. "Once he gets something in his head, he's like a dog with a bone. He won't let it drop."

At the mention of dog, Leo's attention flipped to the puppies again. "I'm asking for one of ol' Maisey's pups when I write to Santa Claus. Then I'll get one for sure. Right, Mom?" He stared up at her with his heart in his eyes.

She started to shake her head while trying to come up with a way to let him down gently when Noah stopped her.

"Santa only answers the wishes of children who are good. So, if you want him to hear you, you know what to do, right?" He met her gaze and winked. *Winked.*

She tried to ignore the jumble of butterflies swirling in her chest to issue a timely warning. "Sometimes, Santa brings things you need, even if you didn't ask for them. It's important to be grateful, no matter what. Okay?"

Leo nodded, but she could see he wasn't really listening. In his mind, he was probably already picking out names for his new puppy.

She moved closer to Noah. "You shouldn't lead him on. He'll be hurt Christmas morning."

He seemed about to say something, but then changed it to, "What did you think of the Kringles?"

Stunned, she whirled around but the elderly couple had disappeared into the thinning crowd. She looked to see if Noah was teasing her, but he appeared serious. "As in Chris and Mary Kringle?" she asked, just to be certain.

"They're snowbirds. They travel all summer, but always come home in time for winter," he said. "They swear there's nowhere else they'd rather be than Christmas for the holidays."

As she watched the flames flicker and dance, Molly had to agree. This little town was taking hold of her heart, too. Noah lifted a tired Leo into his arms for the trek back to the parking lot.

Or maybe it was the people who lived here.

CHAPTER 10

*N*oah took a break from splitting the cord of wood his neighbor had delivered over the weekend. He sank the axe into the chopping block and wiped a tired hand over his brow. In the distance he could see the Andersons, their newlywed guests, cross-country skiing on the trail he'd groomed through the trees. And off to the side, the Hendersons were taking advantage of the sunny day to skate on the frozen pond with their kids, one boy, and the other a cute girl who'd taken to Molly's son. They'd been too busy with the appearance of their guests to talk much, but he was pleased with her innate ability to make the new arrivals feel at home. Within an hour of their check-ins, Molly had already ascertained their meal preferences, given a guided tour of the house, and handed out brochures she'd made filled with upcoming local activities.

Different than when he'd been forced to handle things himself after his aunt went into the hospital. His heart still ached with the loss. She would have liked Molly and young Leo. They added life to the tired old farmhouse. Empty, dusty rooms, now sparkled with cleanliness, the scent of lemon a welcome change from mildew. Instead of silence, the house rang with laughter. The McCartys were a breath of fresh air.

Blaze lifted his head from his front paws, and gazed at the front door, ears perked. Sure enough, a moment later the door opened, and the object of Noah's thoughts spilled onto the porch in joyful ribbons of color. Molly wore a powder pink parka with a white fur hood framing her gorgeous face, and dark jeans that highlighted long, slender legs. She caught sight of him and lifted her hand in greeting, her smile doing crazy things to his pulse. Leo followed close behind in a neon green snowsuit and toque. The minute Blaze saw him he was on his feet and bounding for the stairs.

"Traitor," Noah muttered, wishing he could do the same. He bent and grabbed some wood to add to his stack near the back door. Turning for another armload he was treated to the vision of Molly's shapely rear in the air as she bowed over for some sticks to give him a hand. He sucked in a rough draft of cold air and immediately started coughing.

Molly straightened—*damn*—and stared at him with furrowed brows. "Are you okay?"

He managed a nod and cleared his throat. "Just a frog in my throat. No big deal."

"You swallowed a frog?" Leo asked, bug-eyed.

Molly laughed. "It's an idiom, kind of like when I say you have ants in your pants. It just means his throat is dry. Maybe you could run into the house and grab Mr. Kincaid a bottle of water?"

Leo started to shake his head, took one glance at the look his mother gave him, and turned for the house, Blaze trailing in his wake.

"And don't forget to take off those boots, I just washed the floor," Molly yelled.

Noah stepped close and took the wood from her arms. Her eyes rivaled the brilliance of the crisp, blue sky, stealing his breath. Tendrils of wavy blond hair wrapped themselves under her delicate chin. He gave into the impulse to brush them away and lingered, her skin as soft as the fur of her hood tickling the back of his hand. She licked her lips, leaving them plump and moist. Kissable. His gaze narrowed, the urge to taste overcoming common sense.

He lowered his head.

She lifted her face like a flower to the sun.

His eyes closed in anticipation.

"Hello there," a voice called out cheerfully.

Noah froze.

Molly stared at him before scrambling to put space between them. Noah's hand fell away, years of self-preservation kicking in to protect his heart from the horror he'd read in her eyes and the nervous smile she gave the Andersons.

"How are the trails?" she asked as they skied closer.

Sandy Anderson laughed. "The trails are great. My technique, on the other hand, could use some help."

Her husband, Doug, pointed his pole toward the tree line. "Nice place you have here. How far back does it go?"

Noah shrugged. "Ten acres, give or take. My aunt kept most of it as natural growth forest, except for the area around the house and pond."

Aunt Betty insisted it was their duty to preserve the land, not destroy it. She'd believed in Albert Einstein's quote. *Look deep into nature, and then you will understand everything better.* "Listen, baby boy," she'd say, "there's peace to be found in a wind's soft sigh, the sweet song of a robin, and gentle sway of the trees—Heaven's cathedrals."

"Ever think of selling?" Doug asked. "This would make prime real estate."

"Never." The answer burst from his chest. This

land was his legacy. All he had left. He'd die before he gave it up.

"I think what Noah means is that he loves his home," Molly said. Noah felt the impact of her glance before she hooked her arm with Sandy's. "You're just in time, the Kringles dropped by with fresh-baked apple pie. It was still warm when they left."

Sandy sighed and closed her eyes in bliss. "That sounds delicious. Lead the way, Doug tuckered me out." She giggled.

"Honey, you haven't seen anything yet," Doug murmured. He wrapped a possessive arm around his bride and proceeded to kiss her breathless.

Noah turned away, his arm clenching the wood he still held. "I have work to do." There was no way he could sit and watch the newlyweds make googly eyes at each other over pie while Molly sat across the table looking so damn beautiful. And unreachable.

"See you at dinner?" she asked, her voice velvet to his senses.

He hesitated, then continued toward the wood pile. "Yeah, I'll be there." He could resist everything except temptation.

He took out his frustrations on the chopping block, his axe shattering thick chunks of spruce with a few pieces of birch thrown in for variety. He was a fool. A loner who preferred to live his life out of the spotlight, away from relationships. Caring. Caring meant pain, at least in his world. He was better off on his own. Alone.

"Here's your water," a timid voice said.

Noah jerked in the middle of a downward swing with the axe and narrowly avoided his leg. Cursing under his breath, he sank the blade in the stump and turned to the kid who stared at him with a mixture of awe and curiosity.

"You're strong," Leo said, holding out a bottle. "Will I ever be able to do that?"

He accepted the drink gratefully. "Sure. When you get older." He twisted the cap off and drank half the bottle in a couple of gulps.

"Will you teach me?" Leo eyed the axe, fascinated.

Noah swallowed wrong and choked.

"You do that a lot, huh?"

He wiped his mouth with his hand and bit back a smile. The kid had balls. Grown men watched what they said around him, but Molly's son... he had no fear. "I seem to, yeah."

"So, will ya? Teach me, I mean?" Leo moved a couple of steps closer to the handle sticking out of the wood.

"Not so fast." He grasped the thin shoulder, then let go just as quick. "Your mom would ground both of us if I let you near that thing. It's dangerous. I don't want you touching it unless I say so, understand?"

Leo looked disappointed but nodded. His attention moved to the tree they'd brought home the previous weekend. It sat in a snowbank, the bottom branches blanketing the snow, the crown tilted as though to see why it was stuck in the bank. "Can we decorate the tree, then? Mom says we have to wait for you."

His instinct was to say no. He didn't want it, any of it, but the kid was staring at him like he was a super-hero, and he couldn't do it. He couldn't take that light and squash it. It meant too much to him.

"Help me carry these sticks to the pile and we'll do it after dinner. Deal?"

Leo's grin warmed his battered heart.

"Deal."

CHAPTER 11

The Hendersons spent most of the afternoon skating, then enjoyed s'mores over a campfire Noah had started after he finished chopping wood. Concerned, Molly broached the subject of fires when they had a private moment.

"Does it bother you?" she asked, setting the tray of marshmallows, chocolate and graham crackers on the picnic table. "I noticed you were... shall we say, careful, around the Kringles' firepit the other night."

He glanced up from making a teepee out of sticks, his gaze mocking. "You don't think I have a reason?"

Molly flushed. "Of course, you do. That's not what I meant." She crouched nearby and handed him some newspaper. "It's just that I'm perfectly capable of starting a fire. My dad made sure all of us could handle ourselves outdoors. Not that you'd know it with the mess I made of my car."

"All of you? Just how many McCartys are there?" He squinted and glanced around as though expecting them to stream out of the woods.

She smiled, amused by his discomfort. "Six siblings. I have two brothers and three sisters. I'm the middle child. My dad was a scout leader. We went to camp every summer until we were teenagers and old enough to get jobs."

The fire took hold, burning up the side of the teepee with a bright flare of orange gold. Noah fed a few more sticks to the pile and heat began to radiate outward. Molly held her hands toward the flames and embraced the welcoming warmth, then gasped when a muscular arm cut across her body pushing her away from the pit. She overbalanced and sprawled onto her butt.

"Hey," she cried. Her scowl slowly died at Noah's grim expression. She ignored the hand he held out, scrambled to her feet, and dusted off her backside. "You could have just said something," she grumbled. He'd been protecting her. The indignation she'd felt evaporated, leaving a tingling in her breast that had nothing to do with the fire. "I'm sorry, I should have realized."

"I didn't mean to hurt you." Noah fingered his

scarred lip then glanced toward the Hendersons, laughing and skating without a care in the world.

Hurt her? The only thing hurt was her pride. "It's okay. I shouldn't lean over flames anyhow, that's how accidents happen." She looked at his strong jaw, the deformity caused by the burns only adding to his attractiveness. He was a survivor. She shivered, imagining the pain and horror of that night.

"Are you cold?" he asked, already removing his denim jacket to settle the heavy weight on her shoulders. He tugged the edges of the wool collar together under her chin and retained his grip. "Better?" His voice dropped an octave. Intimate. Sexy.

"Much," she whispered, caught up in this man's undeniable charisma. He'd cut his hair recently, and now it reminded her of a seal's pelt with its coffee-colored hues accenting a broad forehead, intelligent dark eyes and a strong neck.

"Leo says you agreed to put up the tree tonight. Are you sure? I know this must be a tough Christmas for you."

His lips tightened, and he let her go. Even as her heart mourned the loss, her head told her it was for the best. Neither one of them was in a good place to be thinking about a relationship. And their partnership compounded the problem.

"It's fine," he stated. The male equivalent of *what-*

ever. "Life goes on, right? These kids," he nodded toward the Henderson children taking off their skates, "deserve to enjoy the holiday even if I can't."

He was a good man. His road hadn't been an easy one, but he still retained an innate kindness, even if it was covered by a gruff exterior.

Impulsively, she tugged on his arm and reached up to kiss his cheek. "Thank you," she murmured as the kids raced up the path from the pond, their parents trailing behind with knowing smiles. And then they were there, oohing and ahhing over the s'mores, and the private moment was gone. Molly pretended not to regret the loss.

THE CONVERSATION at the dinner table was lively. Molly had somehow found the time to cook a pot roast, complete with mashed potatoes, seasonal vegetables and fresh dinner rolls. Dessert consisted of pumpkin pie or apple crisp. Noah finished his pie, set the fork on his plate and rested, more content than he'd been in a very long time.

The children, done with their supper, had retired to the den to impatiently wait on the adults to decorate the tree. Surprisingly, he didn't mind the thought. He'd moved the crooked balsam to its stand in the living room after the skate party this afternoon leaving time for it to thaw, and already a spicy, minty scent permeated the house.

"Oh, he's a beauty." Ruby Henderson gushed over a photo on Sandy Anderson's cell phone. "Look at those colors."

Sandy handed the phone to Molly. "He wasn't impressed with us interrupting his solitude."

Molly shifted in her seat and leaned against Noah's shoulder so she could show him the photo. The brush of her hair tickled his cheek, her warm weight distracting him from the conversation. He turned his head and their breaths mingled. Her eyes darkened, awareness lancing between them like an electric surge.

"Did you ever see anything so blue?" Ruby asked.

"Never," Noah murmured, his attention never straying from Molly.

"I think she's talking about the jay," she murmured.

"Hmm?"

She held up the phone and he dragged his gaze away from her face long enough to see the photo of a blue jay glaring at the camera from the branch of an aspen tree. Amused, he took the phone and dutifully admired the shot.

"Looks like he wasn't impressed with your photography session," he said, handing the device back. "Their screech is deafening."

Doug nodded. "So we found out. Didn't take us long to ski out of his territory, I'll tell you."

Everyone had a good laugh, then Molly rose to remove the dishes. Noah stood too, reluctant to leave her alone with the chore. Just as he picked up his plate a loud crash came from the den. He looked at Molly's startled gaze, set the dish down, and rushed from the room, concern for Leo causing his heart to pound.

Just as he'd figured, the tree lay on its side, a puddle of water already spreading from the stand. The kids were clustered near the crown, staring at something on the floor. They looked up, frightened when they saw him in the doorway.

He spotted Leo laying awkwardly on the floor and his heart leaped into his throat. "What happened?" he growled, hurrying across the room in three long strides. He crouched by Leo's head and the other kids backed away.

"He... he fell. We didn't mean to break it, Mister. We didn't." The little girl started to sob.

The adults had entered the room by now and were gathered around them. Molly dropped to her knees beside her son and scooped him into her arms. "Oh, Leo. How could you? You could have been seriously injured."

Leo's terrified gaze was fixed on Noah, his eyes too big for his face. "I'm sorry," he whispered. "I'm sorry."

It was only a tree. Noah was more concerned about the child. Thank God he didn't seem...

Molly held up the tattered body of his aunt's Christmas angel, the wings mangled and missing an arm.

Memories swamped him. His aunt's off-key singing as she handed him the handmade decorations they'd done together sitting at her kitchen table. The times she'd rocked him to sleep after he'd woken up crying from nightmares of the fire and the loss of his parents. All the little things she'd done to open her home to a lonely little boy. One who'd been too scared to tell her how much she meant to him until it was too late—she was gone.

And now, so was her angel.

He rose and walked out of the room, leaving a deathly silence in his wake.

CHAPTER 12

*M*olly sat on the side of Leo's bed and watched over him until he fell asleep. He sported a bump on the back of his head, but otherwise had escaped unharmed from the escapade. Apparently, he'd wanted to surprise her with the tree topper so the three kids had come up with the ingenious idea of stacking a stool on top of a chair. Since Leo was the youngest, and the smallest, they'd voted for him to climb the makeshift ladder. It went well until he had to stretch to place the angel on the crooked branch and it wouldn't stay. When it fell, he looked down, got scared, grabbed the tree for support, and toppled over.

She hadn't seen Noah since the accident. He'd been as concerned as she was for Leo. She'd seen it in his expression and the careful way he'd checked her son for injuries. But the ruined angel had destroyed him. She felt horrible. Obviously, it held a special significance for him. In the morning she'd take a closer look and see if there was a way to repair the damage.

Sighing, she leaned over, gently brushed back the fine hair so like his father's and kissed Leo's forehead. He murmured in his sleep, then rolled over and clutched Boo to his side. Her heart clenched. It wouldn't be long before the tattered teddy bear ended up stuffed on a shelf and sports gear would fill the floor. Her boy was growing up.

Molly shut off the bedside lamp and made sure his nightlight filled the room with dinosaur images, then slipped out, leaving the door cracked so she could hear him if he needed her in the night.

The closed door at the opposite end of the hall beckoned and a moment later she stood in front of its wooden panels, her hand raised to knock. Except, what could she say? Too much had happened to Noah. He'd closed himself off and she didn't know how to reach him.

Maybe, he wouldn't want her to try.

Her fingers brushed the cool wood before she turned away. Their relationship had barely started, she hardly knew him, and yet, the loss was keen.

As though her thoughts had called him to her, the

door opened and Noah faced her, his eyebrow raised. "Problem?"

Now that he was there, shirtless and rumpled-looking, she was tongue-tied. Farm life suited him. Her mouth dried as she took in the thick neck and shoulders, powerful arms and delineated abdominal muscles.

"Molly?"

Oh boy, the way he said her name... Butterflies danced in her stomach.

"Molly, what's wrong?" He reached out and drew her into his room, closing the door.

Dark furniture, hard wood floors and a king-sized bed dominated the space. She focused on their clasped hands and frowned, fighting to retain a sense of normalcy. "Actually, I was going to ask *you* that question." She looked up and caught him eyeing her chest. She flushed and tugged free of his grip. "I was... worried when you disappeared earlier. Leo feels awful. He thinks he ruined Christmas."

Instead of reassuring her, Noah turned away and reached for a black Henley long sleeved shirt. Her breath caught as he slid it over his head, the muscles in his shoulders rippling with strength. "I needed some time. Is he okay? He's lucky you picked a sapling instead of a real tree."

Molly smiled. "It has character. Just wait until we

deco…" She stopped. *If* they decorated. "He has a bump on his head. I kept him awake for a couple of hours just to be safe, but I think his pride was hurt more than anything. He was showing off for the other two children."

Noah's lips quirked. "Or the girl, anyway."

"Umm, he's *five*." She loved the easy banter between them. He had a dry wit she found attractive. There were many things about Noah Kincaid that appealed to her.

"I guess I overreacted," he admitted, his gaze watchful. "The angel meant a lot to me. It was my aunt's."

She nodded, hoping he would share more with her. "She raised you, then? After the…?"

He grimaced and once again touched the scar running down his face like a brand. "Fire? Yeah. There was no one else and she refused to see me end up in the foster system." He gestured to the end of his bed, then sat beside her—close, but not near enough.

He picked up her hand and played with her fingers, the rough callouses sending delicious shivers coursing over her body. "I was about your son's age when it happened." She gasped, her heart hurting for the boy he'd been. "At first, I wasn't sure what was happening. Our house wasn't that big. My bedroom was on the main floor while Mom and Dad slept upstairs." He met her gaze and smiled. "She didn't trust me not to sleepwalk, I guess I liked to cause problems even back then."

Molly squeezed his hand. "They loved you."

"Yeah," he snorted, "look where that got them."

She couldn't let him shoulder the blame for another minute without at least trying to ease his pain. She wrapped her arms around his stiff, unyielding frame and whispered, "It brought them peace, Noah."

At first he didn't react, then slowly the tension eased from his shoulders and she felt him let go of years of repressed self-hatred.

He sighed and rested his cheek against hers. "Thank you."

She blinked away tears and continued to hold onto the little boy within the man she'd come to love.

CHAPTER 13

*M*olly was up early the next morning. She'd been unable to sleep after her momentous discovery that she had fallen in love. While Noah had taken a step on the long road to recovery, PTSD was a lifetime battle. If it was only herself... Molly had a child to protect. She didn't for one second think Noah would intentionally harm a fly, but the moods were worrisome. Leo was a sensitive boy. He'd already picked up on Noah's animosity and was bothered by it.

She filled her cup with coffee and joined their guests at the round country-style table in the breakfast nook. "What are your plans for today?" she asked, sliding onto the end of the banquette seating. As late as they were into the winter equinox, the sun had just now peaked over the ridge in the distance. A thin ribbon of pale blue sky drifted across the horizon on either side—lovely, a chinook was on the way. Perfect snowman weather.

"We read your brochure. The kids want to see the giant thirty-five-foot Santa Claus, and then we promised we'd stop by the post office so they could mail their friends cards postmarked from Christmas." Ruby smiled and stole a piece of bacon off her husband's plate. He grimaced, but good-naturedly turned the plate so she could reach the rest more easily.

"We saw a library downtown and thought we'd stop by and read up on the town's history," Sandy said, reaching over to brush her husband's mouth in a lingering kiss. "Doug is fascinated by the iron kilns we passed on the way into town. It looks as though it might have been a big operation at one time."

"It was," Noah murmured, nudging Molly with his hip.

She glanced up, startled, then sucked in a sharp breath. He'd recently showered and like a typical male, hand-brushed his tobacco-brown hair away from his face—the face he wasn't hiding anymore. The reserve he'd worn like a cloak was gone, revealing chiseled features, high cheek bones, thick, dark brows, and eyes as dark as her coffee.

"Are you letting me in?" he asked, lips quirking.

"Hmm? Oh yeah, sorry." Flustered, she slid over,

allowing him room to settle beside her, thigh to thigh. *Oh, boy.*

"Bay Furnace is on the National Registry of Historical Places," he said. "In its heyday it produced twenty tons of pig iron a day."

"I was wondering what the dock was for. That thing must have handled some big ships." Doug finished his breakfast and pushed his plate aside.

Noah nodded. "Twelve-hundred feet. But then, it takes a good-sized barge to maneuver Lake Superior's temperamental waters."

"Too bad we have to get home before Christmas," Ruby said. "It would be fun to have Christmas at Christmas."

"The grandparents would never forgive us," her husband answered. "Come on, honey, we better go and get packed. We have a long drive ahead of us in the morning."

Ruby sighed and lightly punched his arm. "Slave driver." She stood then surprised Molly with a boisterous hug. "Thank you for the lovely vacation. We had a wonderful time and will be sure to tell all of our friends back home."

"Yes," Sandy piped up. "That goes for us, too. I wish we could stay longer, but our parents want us home for our first holiday together as man and wife." She giggled and made googly-eyes at Doug.

He looked embarrassed and crazy in love at the same time. He smiled and reached out to shake Noah's hand. "Maybe next year it will be your turn. We'll be back."

Molly felt the warm stroke of Noah's glance, then he was returning the handshake. "Your rooms will be here."

There was a flurry of goodbyes as the couples left to begin their last day of activities, leaving an uncomfortable silence in their wake. At least he'd moved to one of the vacated seats, so she could breathe again. Even if she missed his closeness. *The other couples seemed so happy together, that's all.*

She rose and began gathering the breakfast plates, anxious to escape the gloomy thoughts nipping at her emotions.

The roar of an engine climbing the road to the inn stilled her hands. She met Noah's carefully blank expression and her curiosity rose.

"Who could that be?" She wiped her hands on a napkin, then turned for the hall leading to the front door, but he caught her hand. She looked at him, surprised. "Noah, what's going on?"

"I...," he started, then shook his head as though he'd changed his mind. "Your car is done. I asked Artie to deliver it as soon as he could. You know, in case you wanted to leave before the holiday traffic rush."

Stunned, she stared into his eyes. Her heart melted at the loneliness she saw lurking in the shadows. She clasped his beloved face in her hands. "You're not getting rid of us that easily, Noah Kincaid. We're here to stay. That is, if you'll have us?"

She'd done it now. She'd gone and laid her feelings at his feet. Was he going to stomp them into the polished hardwood floor, or would he give their relationship a chance to flourish? She held her breath, waiting for his answer.

Noah remembered watching *How the Grinch Stole Christmas* with his aunt as a boy. He'd been fascinated by the concept of a grumpy, lonely Grinch with a heart two sizes too small who terrorizes the village of Whoville on Christmas Eve, stealing all the trees and gifts. But when he learns love is the key to happiness his heart grows three sizes and he returns the gifts to the happy Whos and is invited to participate in the celebrations.

Noah's heart felt like that now. It was surely too big to remain confined within the walls of his chest. How could this beautiful, sweet woman care for him? He'd done nothing but make her life harder since she arrived, and yet... she'd forgiven him.

He gazed into liquid blue eyes and sent a prayer of thanks to his aunt for delivering Molly and her son to a lonely old grouch in need of the gift of love.

"Is that a yes?" she asked, her gorgeous smile wobbling.

He wrapped his arms around her narrow waist and tugged her off her feet. She landed in his lap with a little squeal. "That's a hell yeah," he said just before taking her lips in a kiss guaranteed to steam the windows.

For years the death of his parents had scarred his soul, inside and out, and acted as a brutal reminder of the pain he'd endured. His aunt's death reinforced that belief. That is until one pint-sized boy and his beautiful, tenacious mother stepped in and proved love was a gamble worth taking.

*M*olly opened the oven and inhaled the fragrant scents of rosemary and sage emanating from the fifteen-pound turkey she'd started earlier in the afternoon. She fanned away the heat, then basted the browning bird before closing the range door. Good, dinner should be right on time.

When she'd found out Artie, the collision shop guy, was on his own for Christmas she'd invited him to dinner, which in turn led to invitations to the Kringles and their niece Tammy, from the Roasted Chestnut Café, and Mrs. Nabors, the grocery store clerk. At first, she'd planned a quiet, intimate dinner, just Noah, Leo and herself, but on second thought, this was better. A way to give back to the community and a way for the community to learn about her and Noah.

The flush that climbed from chest to cheeks had

zero to do with the oven and everything to do with the man in the next room. He chuckled at something Leo said and her pulse fluttered. They were getting along so well—it made her heart happy.

"Mom, are you coming?" Leo called.

Smiling, she untied the apron she'd put on to protect her party dress, draped it on the hook by the door, and made her way toward the den. "Hold your horses," she answered, laughing. She entered the room and froze. Noah stood on a ladder, his back to her as he leaned over to wrap a string of multi-colored lights around the misshapen tree. *He looks really good in jeans.*

"Isn't it beautiful? I've been helping lots. Right, Noah?" Her lusty thoughts were interrupted by her son. He jumped up from the array of ornaments spread out across the coffee table, ran to her side and tugged on her arm.

The ladder wobbled, but Noah quickly redistributed his weight and it straightened out. He glanced over his shoulder and gave her a boyish grin. "You didn't see that." He nodded toward the wall switch. "Want to see how they look? Can you reach, buddy?"

Leo broke away and ran for the light switch. He stretched for the lever. "Ready?" he gasped.

"Ready," Noah and Molly said at the same time. The overhead lights went out and the tree was illuminated in all its multi-hued glory. Twinkling prisms of blue, red, green, and white turned the pauper of a tree into a prince. But it was missing an important element.

Molly reached behind the corner chair where she'd hid the repaired angel and handed it to Leo. "Take this to Noah, son."

Leo cradled the ornament in his arms and waited for Noah to descend the ladder. "Mommy fixed this so you could have a happy Christmas, too."

Noah accepted the gift. "Oh, I am," he said, his voice gruff. His eyes shone bright as he looked at Molly. "Thank you."

She smiled and watched him climb back up and carefully set the topper on the tree revealing the glowing figure of an angel, an aura of light radiating from her head. It was the most beautiful tree Molly had ever seen.

Noah descended the ladder and strolled to her side, his head tipped quizzically. "Why the tears?"

She dabbed them away and smiled. "I'm happy, that's all. The angel looks perfect. No wonder your aunt loved her so much."

He opened his arms and she walked right in, contentment warming her belly. "I have a surprise," he murmured.

She tipped her head back and received a lingering

kiss that curled her toes. "I like your surprises," she sighed.

He laughed, and that was a gift, too. She loved to see this side of him, handsome and relaxed.

"Another surprise," he clarified. "Hey, Leo. There's a box with your name under the tree. Do you want to open it?"

"Can I?" Leo jumped up and down. "Please, Mom?"

Dumbfounded that Noah had come up with a gift for her son, Molly nodded. "Just the one. The rest are for Christmas morning."

"Yee-ha," Leo shouted, running across the room to drop down beside a big box wrapped in red paper. He started to rip at the paper, then stopped. A weird expression crossed his face and he backed away from the present. "There's somethin' making noise in there," he whispered.

Noah chuckled and kissed Molly on the nose before moving to crouch beside the box. "C'mere, buddy. I'll help you."

Leo looked nervously at Molly, then edged closer to Noah. "So you know what's in there?" he asked.

Noah grinned. "I'd better. I wrapped it. Come on, kid. You're going to love it, trust me." He lifted one edge of the loosely wrapped top and a paw appeared.

Leo's jaw dropped. "It's a puppy," he cried. Now

that he knew what was waiting, he tore into the box with enthusiasm and soon a fluffy white head with floppy ears appeared. Happy he was free, the pup bounded out of his temporary cage and raced around the room, bumping into chairs and tables in his excitement. Leo laughed and clapped his hands before throwing himself into an unsuspecting Noah's arms. "Thank you. Oh, thank you. This is the bestest gift ever." Then he jumped up and took off chasing the puppy while Blaze looked on from his place near the fire with lazy interest.

Molly would have laughed at the befuddled look on Noah's face, but she was too busy doing the same thing her son had done—running into the arms of the man who'd given *her* the bestest gift of all—love.

PREVIEW SILVER BELLS

JACQUIE BIGGAR

CHAPTER ONE

Christy Taylor smiled at the teens performing skate-board tricks on a set of iron rails, the screech-scrape of their wheels a musical accompaniment to the slap-slap of her sneakers hitting the pavement as she jogged past. Though it was early December on Vancouver Island the sun sat like a warm treat on her shoulders. Snowberries lined the pathway on the Goose Walking Trail, crunching beneath her feet. The unparalleled beauty of the Pacific Ocean lay off to her right. A salty breeze carried the scents of wood, brine, and soil to clear the fog from her brain. The past couple of years had been tough. Between Jill's illness and the increasing costs in rent it was a never-ending battle to keep everything afloat.

She followed the snaky course through Beacon Hill Park, dodging dogs and children and couples holding hands. At the boat pond a father patiently taught his young son how to run the remote control for a jaunty red sailboat, while Mallard ducks paddled nearby searching for scraps.

She turned left and took the path that led her to the seawall, her favorite part of the run.

And there he was.

Every time she'd come by here for the past two

months the same man crouched on the furthest edge of the breakwater, staring out to sea.

He captivated her.

She'd sit on the little spit of sand several feet away and create stories in her head about him. Maybe he was a Russian prince cast out of his homeland. Or a spy waiting on a boat bringing him information meant to save the world. Or maybe even a merman cast upon the shore and unable to find his way back to his watery home. The last brought a wry smile to her lips. Her mom always said she had a writer's imagination.

She opened her fanny pack and drew out a bottle of water, a strip of homemade peach fruit leather, and her drawing supplies. She loved capturing nature on paper with nothing more than a few graphite pencils in varying grades and Caran d'Ache Luminance colors for shading. Her art was slowly gaining recognition, though it was taking more time than she could afford.

Sunset gradually lightened the horizon from chilly winter's grey-blue to neon orange, brilliant fuchsia, and canary yellow. Nimble fingers flew over the page, eager to catch every nuance as it occurred. Her unsuspecting model never moved, his silhouette perfectly captured by the dying rays of the sun.

When it became too dark to draw, Christy set the pad aside and twisted the cap off her water bottle. The liquid was a benediction going down her parched throat. She drank most of it before replacing the lid with a satisfied sigh. The day hadn't begun well, but at least it was ending on a high note. She felt good about the work she'd just produced. It would be easier to tell after she returned to the shop and finished the shading of course, but she was off to a decent start.

Shivering a little now the sun had gone down, she returned everything to the bag and zipped it closed, then stood and brushed the sand from her butt and thighs before bending to pick up the fanny pack. Time to head home, her daughter would be waiting.

A pair of dark brown hiking boots—size enormous —came into her line of sight. Her heart skipped a beat. Most people on the island were friendly, but she *was* a woman on her own, and it was rapidly becoming dark. How stupid.

She tightened her grip on the bag and cursing the fact she'd been so irresponsible, slowly rose to her feet, her gaze following the long, clean line of jean-clad legs, dark cotton shirt, tucked in and belted at the waist, open leather jacket, and chiseled jawline covered in a day's worth of stubble. Glittering eyes stared at her from a deeply tanned, aloof-looking face.

"Quit following me." The voice matched his visage, cold, harsh, and unforgiving.

So much for her fantasy hero. Christy stiffened and glared. "Kind of full of yourself, aren't you?"

He leaned back and crossed his arms, his stance unforgiving. And to think she'd found him intriguing. Ha, more like infuriating.

"So it's just a coincidence every time I turn around, there you are?" He lifted a hand and rubbed the back of his neck. The rasping sound along with the backdrop of the swishing waves made her —restless.

"Look, I don't do interviews, okay? Not even for cute little pixies. Tell your boss, next time I'll call the cops."

Incredulity overrode her apprehension. "Are you serious? I have as much right to be on this beach as you do, buddy. Trust me, you're not half as fascinating as you seem to think you are."

In between one breath and the next, Mr. Personality seized the bag out of her grip and delved inside.

"Hey, give that back," she cried, trying to wrestle it out of his grasp.

"If you have nothing to hide..." He pulled the drawings free and turned his wall of a back on her.

Christy couldn't believe this was happening. Adrenaline zipped through her body, leaving her feeling more alive than she had in a long while. And it was all due to this... this jerk ripping pages out of her workbook while she stood by helpless to do anything about it. All that work—gone.

"Please," she begged, her throat husky. "I meant no harm. I draw for a living. That's all they are, drawings."

At least the shredding stopped.

He leveled his gaze on her again, as though deciding whether to throw the whole bag out to sea or not. She really hoped not. It had taken months to save for those pencils. They were the very best and made a huge difference to the level of her workmanship.

"Please," she said again.

He hesitated, then folded the sheets of paper he'd taken and shoved them into his jacket pocket before handing over her bag.

"Next time you might try asking," he said dryly.

As he clumped away in those heavy boots his voice floated back to her on the breeze. "The answer would've been no, by the way."

Was it too much to ask that he trip over his enormous—arrogance?

AFTERWORD

Reviews are the lifeblood of any successful author. Without you, we can't be heard.

If you enjoy the story, please consider sharing on your favorite social media sites, as well as GoodReads and from wherever you've bought the book.

Thank you,

Jacquie Biggar

Jacqbiggar.com

JACQUIE BIGGAR is a USA Today bestselling author of Romantic Suspense who loves to write about tough, alpha males and strong, contemporary women willing to show their men that true power comes from love.

She is the author of the popular Wounded Hearts series and has just started a new series in paranormal suspense, Mended Souls.

She has been blessed with a long, happy marriage and enjoys writing romance novels that end with happily-ever-afters.

Jacquie lives in paradise along the west coast of

Canada with her family and loves reading, writing, and flower gardening. She swears she can't function without coffee, preferably at the beach with her sweetheart. :)

Sign up now to keep up with Jacquie's new releases, excerpts, giveaways, and more:

Newsletter

jacqbiggar.com
jbiggar@jacqbiggar.com

ALSO BY JACQUIE BIGGAR

WOUNDED HEARTS SERIES

Tidal Falls

The Rebel's Redemption

Twilight's Encore

The Sheriff Meets His Match

Summer Lovin'

Wounded Hearts Box Set

Maggie's Revenge

With This Heart

MENDED SOULS SERIES

The Guardian

The Beast Within

Virtually Gone

GAMBLING HEARTS

Hold 'Em

Crazy Little Thing Called Love

My Girl

Married to The Texan- Box set

BLUE HAVEN

Sweetheart Cove

Sunset Beach

MEN OF WARHAWKS

Skating on Thin Ice

The Player

SINGLE TITLES

Silver Bells

The Lady Said No

My Baby Wrote Me A Letter

Tempted by Mr. Wrong

Valentine: A Hearts and Kisses Romance

Mistletoe Inn

The Sister Pact

Perfectly Imperfect

www.ingramcontent.com/pod-product-compliance
Lightning Source LLC
Chambersburg PA
CBHW060940120626
46557CB00003B/1085